Happy Trails!

♡ Robin H Kramer

Mulberry
Dreams

ROBIN H. KRAMER

ARCHWAY
PUBLISHING

This is a work of fiction. All of the characters, names, incidents,
organizations, and dialogue in this novel are either the products
of the author's imagination or are used fictitiously.
Archway Publishing books may be ordered
through booksellers or by contacting:

Archway Publishing
1663 Liberty Drive
Bloomington, IN 47403
www.archwaypublishing.com
1 (888) 242-5904

Because of the dynamic nature of the Internet, any web
addresses or links contained in this book may have changed
since publication and may no longer be valid. The views
expressed in this work are solely those of the author and do
not necessarily reflect the views of the publisher, and the
publisher hereby disclaims any responsibility for them.

Any people depicted in stock imagery provided by Thinkstock are
models, and such images are being used for illustrative purposes only.
Certain stock imagery © Thinkstock.

ISBN: 978-1-4808-4707-1 (sc)
ISBN: 978-1-4808-4708-8 (e)

Library of Congress Control Number: 2017907081

Print information available on the last page.

Archway Publishing rev. date: 05/05/2017

Contents

In memory of my parents,
Bob and Dorothy Kramer,
who filled my childhood years
with joy, hope, and love

Chapter 1

Animal Friends

Storm clouds hovered over the farm, and distant sounds of rolling thunder shook the air. Hilary lay stretched out over her pony's back beneath the twin mulberry trees, lazily looking up at the plump, purple berries and hoping one would drop down to her. Her pony, Holly, stood quietly and patiently as usual. Her round rump was the perfect pillow for Hilary's head. Often Hilary brought her deepest thoughts to these two twisted mulberry trees, perhaps hoping for some sort of answer. She loved her pony more than anything, but she knew that her family might have to sell Holly when Hilary outgrew her as a rider.

Soon those thoughts were punctuated with distant calls from her father urging Hilary to return to the stable. "The storm's coming, and you need to get back! Now!" And before Hilary could gather the reins, Holly started to turn and perk up her ears toward his call.

The rain came all at once. Sometimes even during a bright, sunny day such as this, the south Florida rain comes in torrents and drenches the parched ground, only to have the sun dry it again quickly by day's end. Hilary rode her pony to beat the rain, racing across the grassy field, past the house, the goat's pen, the water trough, and the chicken coop. Rain fell off the backs of the horses in the field, but they kept their heads down, grazing intently. Mr. Andrews and several children were gathered at the door to the barn.

By the time she reached the barn doors, Hilary and Holly were soaked. The children parted to the sides to let them enter. "Not much warning," he said with a laugh. "You look like a wet rat!" She slid off her pony as he wrapped her in a warm, dry towel.

The old barn weathered many storms over the years. It was made of white painted concrete with forest green wooden trim. The two wooden sliding doors opened to a wide center aisle, and there were two rows of spacious stalls, one for each horse. Each stall had a screened window, and the shutters could be pulled closed in case of a hurricane. It was cool in the summer and warm in the winter. The smell of fresh hay and grain filled the air, and since it was near feeding time, the horses, hoping for an apple, a carrot, or perhaps some spilled grain within their reach, poked their heads over the stall guards. Rusty, rolling wheels on the wheelbarrow could be heard as buckets rattled and horses nickered softly. Hilary thought the barn had a peaceful rhythm. It was a place where nothing bad could ever happen and where dreams became real.

After drying off her pony, Hilary put Holly into her stall, wiped off the wet bridle, and walked back to the tack room, where all sorts of riders were chatting about their riding lessons and horses. The aroma of leather and saddle soap filled the room. Because she was the oldest daughter, Hilary was given more responsibilities on the farm: helping feed and water the horses, saddling them, assisting younger children in learning to ride, and sweeping the barn. She arranged the bridles on their hooks just so, cleaned the tack room, answered the barn phone, and did whatever chores needed to be done. Hilary's long, wavy ponytail, held by a piece of yarn or rubber band, was usually full of dust, cobwebs, or a lone piece of hay. Her worn jeans and worn, ratty sneakers showed just how much she lived at the barn.

After school each day, she raced into the house, grabbed a snack—a carrot or an apple—and went straight to the barn. Holly was her favorite. She was a beautiful bay mare with a shiny coat that Hilary brushed lovingly each day. Hilary felt so comfortable with Holly and so safe. But Mr. Andrews had a new horse all picked out. They had raised Chipper since he was a foal. He was a beautiful steel gray with a glorious floating trot and plenty of spunk. Hilary admired the older riders who trained him, and she pictured herself one day riding him in the big South Miami horse show at the fairgrounds. He was not an easy horse to ride, and although Hilary was fearless in many ways, riding was not one of them. She anxiously awaited the day that Chipper would become her own and she would have to give up Holly to someone else.

Will he ever be as easy to ride as Holly? she thought. *Will I ever be able to ride him up to the mulberry trees or bareback or race across the field?*

"We have to be practical about these things," said Mrs. Andrews. "Holly would be the perfect pony for children who are afraid to ride—and your legs are hanging down to her knees when you ride her."

"She's helped to make you a better rider, too," she added. The farm was also a riding school, so calm, steady horses and ponies were always in demand.

"I know," replied Hilary. "It's just that I love that pony so much."

Mrs. Andrews was a sensible woman and the best mom in the whole world. She wore plaid shirtwaist dresses and sandals every day. She never wore makeup or perfume, and she always smelled like the fresh outdoors. No matter what the problem, she had a solution. Hilary was hesitant to admit to her parents that she was more than a little afraid to ride Chipper.

She thought about the first time she'd ridden bareback on Holly and how it seemed so easy. If she'd fallen off, she wouldn't have had far to go. It was much less frightening to canter around the paddock with her friends, doing flying dismounts and riding backward. Her pony also listened to voice commands. With a whispered whoa, Holly would stop instantly. In the back field behind the barn, a course of jumps was set up so that riders could practice. Holly was so well trained that she rarely stopped at a jump, bucked, or gave Hilary any problems. Her pony made Hilary feel fearless and confident. They were a perfect pair.

Saturdays and Sundays during the school year were great. After Hilary completed her farm chores of helping feed, water, and hay the horses, she was free to do as she pleased. She always rode her pony three or four times on the weekends, cleaned and polished her saddle and bridle, and often gave Holly a sudsy bubble bath. Often this left Hilary just as wet and soapy as her pony.

Of Hilary's two younger sisters, Franny and Sara, Franny was the youngest. She was energetic, good-natured, and fearless. She was often seen riding around the farm bareback, just looking for something daring to do. Her tangled dirty-blonde curls went bouncing down her back, just as free as she. Franny's tan, freckled face was always smiling, and her laugh was contagious. Everyone loved Franny's good-hearted nature.

Once, Franny found a box of kittens at the front gate. Upon watching them wobble on their shaky little legs, she scooped up the five balls of fuzz. She promptly claimed the kittens as her own and took care of them for weeks. They became barn cats, and Franny named each one.

The character of Sara, the middle sister, was the opposite of Franny's tomboyish nature. Sara loved to sing and perform, and she had a vivid imagination. Her room was filled with dolls, stuffed animals, and every sort of craft imaginable. She loved to paint her nails, and she wore her shoulder-length brown hair with style. Sara smelled of rose lotion, and she loved going to Grandma's to sit at her vanity mirror, trying on jewelry and makeup. When the girls went to their grandparents' house, Hilary and Franny usually went outside to play while Sara helped Grandma bake cookies and cut coupons.

Sara loved the farm too and the three sisters felt very lucky indeed. People often dropped off animals at the farm, which had become a haven for lost and abandoned creatures. And on weekdays after school, the farm was flooded with kids taking riding lessons, playing with the animals, or helping with the barn chores.

Chapter 2

The Witch Next Door

Hilary found her mom in the kitchen of their old farm-house. The kitchen was small, with matching, some-what chipped, white appliances and old worn-out beige wooden cupboards. Soft yellow wallpaper with tiny daisies covered one wall. An old metal breadbox sat on one end of the counter, and the aroma of coffee filled the air.

"What's for homework tonight?" asked Mrs. Andrews.

"Well, just some math problems to do," replied Hilary, plopping herself onto the rickety stool near the table.

"Then I'll have time to ride!" she said with a cheer. She sat watching her mother with her elbows on the table and her chin cupped in her hands. The fresh, white goat's milk poured smoothly into the glass container and bubbled at the top. Hilary preferred this to cow's milk, which she sometimes had at school. At milking time, Nanny, the goat, willingly got onto the milking stand, and while she was eating her bucket of sweet feed, Mr. Andrews gathered the day's milk. Now it was being made ready to drink, and there was quite a lot.

"I would love to make raspberry cobbler for dessert tonight, Hil," said her mom. "Would you please go over to Mrs. Peacock's and see if she has a pint of berries for sale?"

"What?" squeaked Hilary. "I just had a great day at school, I'm getting ready to ride, and I thought you asked me to visit the witch's house to get berries."

"Yes, please. And she's not a witch!" said Mrs. Andrews, giving Hilary a look of suspicion.

"Yes she is," whispered Hilary under her breath.

Hilary's best friend, Sally, just happened to come rolling up the driveway on her brand-new purple three-speed bike, yelling, "Hey! Let's go ride the ponies out on the trails." She whizzed right up to Hilary, put on the brakes, skidded to a halt, and hopped off the bike.

"I can't," Hilary replied. "I have to go and get raspberries from the witch next door."

"Wait, I *really* want to go, too!" cried Sally. Sally was way braver about all things in life, and that was one of the reasons Hilary liked her so much. Sally had what Hilary wished she had—courage. She was a tall, spindly girl with long, straight blonde hair, great green eyes, and a laugh that made Hilary smile just thinking about it. And because of her long legs, the kids sometimes called her Spider Legs.

Sally leaned over to offer the last of her apple to Fitz, one of the Andrews family pets. Dogs don't usually eat apples, but he gobbled it up like a pig, without a trace of enthusiasm, as if he was doing her a favor.

"That dog will eat anything," Sally reminded Hilary.

"C'mon, we can ride bikes over to the witch's house." And off they went, gliding down the gravel driveway.

Mrs. Peacock lived in a little stone house covered with vines next door to the Andrews farm, and most of the children were afraid of her. On her front door hung an old wreath full of cobwebs, dust, and yellow silk begonias that looked brittle and worn. Nearby, herbs grew in terra-cotta pots, looking for an escape from their ancient, cracked homes. Behind the cottage was a magnificent garden, mostly filled with red raspberry bushes, and Mrs. Peacock was often found stooped over, gently tickling the berries into her bucket. Maybe it was the scruffy black cat in her window or the old-fashioned straw broom on her doorstep that did it. She was a frail old woman whose scowling face made her seem even more intimidating. When she found children spying on her, which they sometimes did, she gave them a look that instilled fear and trembling.

Usually, Mrs. Andrews visited Mrs. Peacock, or sometimes Hilary just left some money in the old, rusted, red coffee can on her porch after grabbing a carton of berries. But now she actually had to talk to the woman. Hilary was glad to have Sally with her. They stopped their bikes, put down the kickstands, and slowly approached the picket fence near the front of the house. The fence was high—about six feet—but cracked and worn in places. Sally hoisted Hilary up so that she could see over the fence. With a small, shaky voice, Hilary cried, "Hello, may I buy some raspberries today?"

"Louder!" said Sally. "She can't hear you."

Hilary repeated her words. Mrs. Peacock was intent in her work, hunched over her sweet berries, her wispy gray hair framing her worn, wrinkled face. Finally she looked up and approached the girls. Her thin, faded floral dress was sagging to her knees and had blotches of red stains all over the front.

"It's probably blood," whispered Sally.

"Not funny!" hissed Hilary. Mrs. Peacock carried an old tin bucket and looked as though she could barely make it to where they stood. Her thin lips were set in a straight line, and her wrinkles were even more evident up close. Both girls were now standing on the ground on the other side of the fence, glued to the spot.

"What's that? Speak up," called Mrs. Peacock.

"I'm sorry to bother you, but my mom sent me over for some berries, if you have a spare pint," Hilary said.

Mrs. Peacock told the girls to go around to the front and go ahead into the kitchen. There were berries on the counter, and they could leave the money there.

"Who in their right mind goes into a witch's house?" whispered Hilary.

"We do!" cried Sally, and in they went.

The door squeaked on its hinges and opened into a dark, damp-smelling kitchen, with pots hanging from the ceiling and an old gas stove with the pilot light burning. The girls wondered what went into those pots. Were they for boiling things like snakes, snails, and cockroaches? Dust had collected on the shelves, and woven curtains kept the light from shining in. The old counter held burn marks and cracks from years ago. The girls stood hushed and motionless. How still and empty the house felt. Inside there was not a sound except the ticking of the clock and their own breathing.

"Let's make this quick," said Hilary.

She spied the cartons of berries, filled to the brim, and quickly gathered one up, leaving the money in its place.

Suddenly, a loud creak came from above the pantry and something pounced right over the girls' heads, catching Sally's long, golden hair on the way down! It was the cat! He arched his back and bristled his tail, hissing and spitting at them. Hilary still held the carton of berries, but then the girls took off in a mad dash for the door. The cat chased after them, flying off the old cane rocker in the living room and snarling all the way. The screen door slammed, Hilary threw the berries into her bike basket, and they sped off, their legs pedaling as fast as they could. Bike baskets banging and raspberries bouncing out of the carton, they flew down the road.

"This raspberry cobbler better be well worth it!" cried Hilary.

But Sally didn't hear her. She was already halfway up the Andrews driveway.

"Did you get the berries?" Mrs. Andrews asked cheerfully.

"Yes!" the girls cried in unison.

"And please don't ever ask us to do it again," said Hilary.

Sally handed the semi-smashed berries to Hilary's mom, her hands still trembling.

The girls ran to the barn to tack up their horses and ride. Hilary had started taking lessons on Chipper with her instructor, Jenny, two weeks ago. Every day they practiced in the small ring: posting trot, slow sitting trot, cantering, with and without stirrups.

"Hilary, try to relax and he will relax, too," called Jenny.

"I think we should *not* drop our stirrups," suggested Hilary.

Jenny laughed, "Good try, but I think *we* should."

"It's great for your balance, your seat, and your legs." They practiced, and Chipper was a bit faster than Holly, but he responded well to her commands.

Jenny was Hilary's favorite riding instructor. She came to the farm at sunrise most days, wearing her floppy straw hat. Slender in her tucked-in shirt and worn jeans, she wore brown laced riding boots. Jenny had one long braid that sprouted from the back of her hat, and she often smelled like coconut suntan lotion. She was soft-spoken and gentle, a terrific rider and teacher. She was amiable, and no one ever saw her frown or heard her speak a cross word. If anyone could help Hilary overcome her fear of riding Chipper, it would be Jenny.

When they were unsaddling their horses, Sally said, "Wait until we tell the kids at school about the witch!"

"Monday comes too quickly," said Hilary. The girls attended Pinewood Elementary as fourth graders. Hilary had few friends other than Sally, and she wasn't looking forward to their third week of school. She wished she could just stay home and ride.

Chapter 3

The Meat Loaf Sandwich

At Pinewood Elementary, Hilary's fourth grade teacher was Mrs. Simpson, a lovely woman whose mousy brown hair was full of curls. She always wore buttoned-up dresses with a belt, sensible shoes, and stockings. Hilary loved everything about her, especially the way she read stories aloud to the class each day. She had a huge Mason jar of sour balls on her desk, as much for herself as for the students, Hilary guessed. Anyone who scored 100 percent on a reading test could choose any color sour ball. Hilary always chose red, which tasted like sweet, tart cherries. Her teacher was her favorite thing about school. Sally was not in Hilary's homeroom class, but they did have math class together.

In her class were two not-so-nice girls who teased Hilary behind her back and sometimes right to her face. They were from the nearby neighborhood of Pine Grove, with fancy houses, manicured lawns, and shrubs trimmed with the same precision as those at the royal palace. The rest of the area was developed with communities like Pine Grove.

The Andrews farm was fourteen acres of pasture, with two big ficus trees, southern pines, some fruit trees, and a few oak trees. Florida holly grew wild, and the riding ring fence posts were dotted with goldenrod. It was one of the few farms left in the southwest part of Miami and just a few miles north of the Florida Everglades. Hilary's life was quite different than her friends, who had sidewalks, paved streets, and fewer natural places to play.

But these two girls thought they were beautiful and oh so very smart. They wore the most fashionable dresses and shoes, carried brand new lunch bags with individual containers for each item in their lunch, and they always brought flavored bottled water. Bracelets dangled on their wrists, and they wore matching nail polish. They made fun of Hilary's plain clothing, her hair, and her plain lunches. Sometimes they neighed or clucked like a hen and called her a country bumpkin in passing or held their noses. And what made Mimi and Sherry most unappealing was that they disliked Mrs. Simpson. They talked and giggled during lessons and made fun of others too. Hilary silently ignored them, but it began to get worse.

Hilary looked forward to seeing her mom or dad at the end of the school day. When her mom came to pick her up in the station wagon, it was fine. Sometimes they stopped at the grocery store on the way home or the local convenience store to get a slushy. There were times when her mom needed to stay at the farm, so Hilary's dad would come at the end of the school day. He would drive up that circular driveway in his old pea green Ford pickup truck. It made rattling noises, the paint was peeling, and it was clearly a farm truck. Worst of all, when Mr. Andrews drove over the speed bumps too fast, sprays of compost would fly out of the sides and back of the truck, settling on any unsuspecting passersby.

Once he whipped past Mimi's mother, Mrs. Moore. With a look of disgust and horror, and with sprigs of hay on her perfect pink suit, she yelled out, "Why don't you leave that filthy truck at the farm?"

Mr. Andrews didn't hear her but just smiled and waved. Hilary stepped up on the running board and climbed into the truck of shame. But then, seeing her dad's cheerful smile, inhaling the fresh scent of hay, and thinking about her animals, Hilary quickly forgot about the humiliating exit. She talked to him about her day at school and told him about the two girls that were rude to her and others. His advice was to "rise above it" and continue to treat others with respect, and maybe they would eventually see the error in their ways. He was probably right, but it helped only a little. Then one day something happened that made her dad take notice.

When Hilary's mom packed her lunch, it was usually peanut butter and jelly or bologna, cheese, and mayo. She also included a piece of fruit and a cookie. Hilary often bought milk from the school cafeteria. One week her mom decided to send meat loaf sandwiches since they had leftovers from Sunday's dinner. They were delicious on wheat bread with catsup. She had them two days in a row, but on the third day Hilary noticed that her sandwich was missing from her brown bag lunch. Although she was very hungry, she said nothing and ate the pear and oatmeal cookie.

Just after lunchtime, Mimi and Sherry walked past Hilary and said, "Yum, lunch was delicious, wasn't it Hilary?" They said it in the most rude way, with smirks on their faces.

The next day Hilary brought the same lunch but still didn't tell her parents what happened because after all she couldn't prove that those two took her sandwich. Hilary found her sandwich missing again. That night when her parents asked her about her day, tears welled up in her eyes and her dad asked what happened. Hilary explained the case of the missing sandwich and told them she suspected Mimi and Sherry, but she wasn't sure.

"What makes you think that?" asked her mom.

"Well, each time part of my lunch was gone they were giggling as they walked past me," cried Hilary.

"I can't prove it," said Hilary, "but they are just mean enough to do something like that."

Mr. and Mrs. Andrews looked at each other, and Mr. Andrews said, "Hilary, I have a plan to outsmart whoever is stealing your lunch." He wore that devious smile that reassured Hilary he was on her side.

They packed a lunch that was, well, fit for a dog. In fact, Fitz was hungrily awaiting his part in the scheme, sitting perfectly still on the tile of the kitchen floor. Mr. Andrews opened a can of dog food and carefully sliced it. Because the contents were nice and firm, this was easy to do. He placed it between two slices of wheat bread, poured on some catsup, cut it corner to corner just the way her mom did, and wrapped it in waxed paper. In the brown bag went an orange, a chocolate chip cookie and the questionable sandwich. In another bag, hidden in her backpack, was an edible sandwich for Hilary to eat at lunchtime.

The next afternoon, when the rattling old farm truck came bouncing over the speed bumps up to Pinewood Elementary, Hilary had a big smile on her face. As she hopped into the truck, she told her dad that the sandwich had been returned to her bag, partially eaten, still in the wax paper. They both laughed out loud, and Hilary's lunch was never stolen again. Hilary's dad was great for this sort of thing. He knew what would work and it did. Perhaps it was her imagination, but Hilary thought that those two girls seemed to be a little more respectful lately.

With a renewed feeling of confidence, Hilary was eager to get back home and practice for the upcoming horse show. Her lessons with Jenny and Chipper were becoming much more comfortable. Hilary could now walk, trot, and canter around the large ring, and she could even change directions while cantering with a simple change of lead. She practiced putting her reins in a knot and letting them rest on Chipper's neck while guiding him with just her legs and seat. She jumped him over low cross rails from a trot and a canter. Jenny was pleased with their progress.

"You've really connected with Chipper," said Jenny.

"He's not as scary as I once thought," admitted Hilary. "I miss Holly, but at least I get to see her every day, and I do think I'm feeling better about riding Chipper."

"Next time, let's try riding him in the back field and do a little more jumping," suggested Jenny.

"Sounds good," said Hilary. But that was a big step forward, and she wasn't sure they were ready for the big, wide-open back field. She trusted Jenny and looked to her for advice. Hilary was still not quite as confident as she wanted to be.

Chapter 4

Fun on Horseback

Riders filled the ring on their horses, getting ready for a group lesson. Jenny was helping one of them check her horse's girth to make sure the saddle was on tight. Hilary helped a rider whose stirrup leathers needed to be shortened. Mrs. Andrews was helping a little girl onto Holly, and Hilary felt a touch of jealousy. Or maybe it was sadness or regret. Whatever it was, she felt it in the pit of her stomach.

"How about checking Holly's bridle?" called Mrs. Andrews to Hilary.

"Okay, Mom," she replied. And then she said to the new rider, "Holly has a slow, smooth gait, and she stops really easily. You just say whoa." The girl smiled, and Hilary wrapped her arms around her pony for a hug. "You'll love riding her," she added. Hilary hopped on Chipper and joined the group.

After the hour-long lesson, the ring was dirty and dusty. Jenny's face was powdered in dust, and the riders walked their horses to the water trough for a drink before dismounting. Back at the barn, Jenny asked Mr. Andrews if he would start the sprinklers before the afternoon lessons.

There were three riding rings on the farm, and around the perimeter of this one water sprinklers jutted up from several posts. Grass no longer grew in the ring, and the hot sun baked the surface. The kids on the farm loved to play with their horses or ponies. On steamy, hot days, they would gallop around the ring with the sprinklers on full blast, riding bareback through the mist. This, of course, made the horses' backs even more slippery. Around and around the ring they'd canter, like an animated merry-go-round at the county fair. The greatest challenge was to ride backward or to stand up on the horses' backs. Holly had a broad back with plenty of padding. That made it easier for Hilary to join in the fun. Sometimes they even rode double bareback. The danger in that was that both riders would fall at the same time if one lost her balance. After that dusty lesson, several riders came back out on their horses to play in the water.

Franny was fearless, especially when it came to riding. She was the youngest of the sisters, but her horse, Cocoa, was the tallest. She would ride Cocoa all around the farm on her little western saddle, pigtails floating in the breeze. She was as carefree as a butterfly, flitting from one thing to the next. When the older kids were playing under the sprinklers, Franny decided to join them. She climbed up on the picnic table, removed the saddle, and hopped right onto Cocoa's back. Cocoa was a palomino mare, with a long flowing mane, who was especially gentle with children. She stood quietly and bowed her head as children crawled on her back or groomed her coat. Franny loved Cocoa with all her heart. She was not a jumper, but she taught many children how to ride over the years.

Franny trotted into the ring and nudged Cocoa into a canter right away. Peals of laughter came from the riders as they watched little Franny sliding around on her horse's back. And then it happened: Fitz came running into the ring to join the fun, barking and chasing the horses' tails. He ran right in front of Cocoa, and she stopped dead in her tracks.

"Grab her mane!" yelled Hilary. But it was too late. Franny slid right down Cocoa's slippery, wet neck, over her head, and plop! right into the muddiest puddle in the ring. The kids rushed over to Franny, who looked like she was taking a mud bath, sitting cross-legged, her pigtails soaked and her clothes drenched in the enormous, muddy mess. Mrs. Andrews came running over and tromped right through the mud to her daughter.

"Are you okay?" she cried as she tried to wipe mud from Franny's face.

"I'm just fine," said Franny. "Now will you please give me a boost up so I can rinse off again?"

Everyone laughed. It was so like fearless Franny to hop right back on her horse. After a little while, the sprinklers were turned off, and the riders and horses dried in the bright Florida sunshine.

Chapter 5

Practice Makes Perfect

After school Hilary rushed to change her clothes, grabbed a bag of carrots, and skipped off to the barn, arriving just in time for her riding lesson.

Jenny was helping Joey adjust his stirrups and called out, "Hi Hilary! I brought Chipper to the cross ties for you."

Hilary gave him a big hug and fed him the last carrot in the bag, which she'd already shared with several horses along the way. Chipper shook his head in delight. After carefully brushing, picking out hooves, and combing his mane and tail, Hilary saddled up and led him out of the barn.

"Today we'll be learning about figure eights and flying lead changes," said Jenny. "We'll also practice jumping the course in the back field."

"Ugh," Hilary said to Joey. "There's a coop in the back field that looks gigantic, and I hope Chipper cooperates."

Joey replied, "I've seen him jump that coop many times."

"Yes, but not with me!" answered Hilary.

Jenny walked the two riders out to the ring where they practiced. Joey was the only boy on the farm, but he didn't seem to mind. He rode with the girls and helped Hilary and her friends clean the stalls. His red, curly hair and face full of freckles made him look just as mischievous as ever.

Each lesson started out in the large ring, working on the flat: walking, trotting, and cantering. Joey and Hilary practiced figure eights at a trot, halting, and backing in the middle. They learned how to do a flying lead change at the canter by shifting their weight and using hand and leg signals. They took turns trotting over the cross rails and circling around as Jenny raised the height of the rails.

"Heels down, eyes up, look ahead," said Jenny, guiding them with her instructions into each jump. "Now it's time to drop your stirrups." Although this was not Hilary's favorite exercise, it was fun to try.

"My legs feel like spaghetti," cried Joey. "When can we stop?"

"Don't make me laugh or I'll bounce right off!" yelled Hilary.

They all laughed out loud as Jenny called them to the center of the ring. They talked about ways to improve their riding and what would be expected at the coming horse show.

They walked their horses out to the back field and trotted around a bit. Then Jenny gave them a course to canter through.

"First jump the brush box, then the cross rails, the picket fence, and end with the coop," instructed Jenny.

"You go first," Hilary told Joey.

"Chicken!" whispered Joey.

So off he went, with his horse cantering lazily around the course and correctly finding each spot before takeoff. Then it was Hilary's turn. The brush box was easy and so were the cross rails because Hilary had spent a long time on those before. Chipper took a wide leap over the picket fence and headed toward the coop at the end of the field.

"C'mon boy, we can do this," whispered Hilary.

She went into her forward seat position … one, two, three … up and over! Thanks to perfect timing and a trustworthy horse, they flew over the coop. The rest of the lesson continued with much the same success. After trying a few more jumps, they walked their horses to cool them down.

Then something startled Chipper. He pranced sideways past the forest of trees that lined the back of the field as Hilary gathered up her reins. For some reason, he was afraid to pass by those looming pine trees, but Hilary urged him forward. With Jenny's guidance, Hilary trotted him around the inner part of the field, his big, bouncy gait so much different than Holly's short, choppy steps. Hilary was tense and Chipper knew it. She wanted to reach down to pat his neck, to tell him it was okay. But she was afraid to let go of even one rein. Hilary thought of all the difficult moments in her riding career that she conquered just by thinking positively. This was another one. She trotted Chipper back and forth past those trees five times. She didn't notice the dark clouds that were gathering overhead or the way the wind had begun to whistle through the trees and how the leaves were turning their backs to the wind. But Chipper could hear and smell the storm coming. He twitched his ears, lowered and raised his head, and started stepping sideways like a Lipizzan stallion. Then Hilary realized that she may be in trouble.

"Come back, come back!" called Jenny. "It's going to storm!"

As if in answer to her cry, there was an ear-splitting clap of thunder, and Chipper turned and bucked straight up in the air. Hilary clung tightly to his mane and sat deeply in the saddle. He lunged forward and galloped away from the trees, and she pulled hard on the right rein to circle him around. Thankfully, he stopped his gallop and pranced in place with nostrils flaring.

"It's only a storm, boy," Hilary said.

Jenny came over and asked her if she wanted to dismount so they could lead Chipper back to the barn.

"I think we'll be okay," answered Hilary. "Just stay nearby." Between walking and jogging back to the barn, Hilary felt like she was in charge. This was one step toward not being a scaredy-cat, she thought. She smiled.

"Way to go!" called Joey.

"Yes," said Jenny. "You should be very proud of yourself. You handled that well."

Hilary's voice quivered a bit as she replied, "Thank you, I'm glad we're back at the barn."

After her horse was cooled down and put away, Hilary stopped by to see Holly.

"I miss you, girl," she whispered. " Don't think I'm deserting you, but I have a lot of work to do with your buddy, Chipper," she said.

Holly put her warm, soft nose in Hilary's pocket, looking for an extra treat as Hilary gave her a great big hug.

Chapter 6

Monkey Business

In addition to the mulberry trees on the farm, there was a beautiful rose apple tree with fruit that smelled as delicious as it tasted. There were also two grapefruit trees and a sea grape tree in the backyard, near the house. Sometimes a friend of Mrs. Andrews would visit to gather the sea grapes and make jelly. But the most beloved tree of all was the giant ficus tree near the barn. Mr. Andrews guessed that the tree was almost one hundred years old. The leaves were smooth, silky, and green with even edges—small leaves for such a monstrous tree. What was most intriguing about the ficus was that its new roots hung from the branches and reached downward to the earth. It was a good climbing tree, with many arms that branched out searching for the sky. There were nooks in which to hide, the perfect place for someone small, like a little monkey.

The coolness under the tree beckoned parents and friends who sat to watch their children take riding lessons. It was a social meeting place, with two oaken Adirondack chairs, the paint peeling on their worn armrests, and a weathered picnic table sharing the spot at the base of the old tree.

Often wandering the farm was a goose named Henrietta, the goats, chickens, assorted dogs, an old pony named Salty, a cat named Velvet, quite a few stray barn cats and kittens that had come over the years, and even a raccoon. There was also a capuchin monkey by the name of Ricky.

Hilary remembered the day that Ricky came to live on the farm. It was a winter day and unexpectedly cold for Miami, as an older couple drove up the driveway in a long, shiny, black car that looked out of place for the farm. As they stepped out, Hilary noticed that the woman wore a furry coat and held a jeweled leash. On its end was the most beautiful little round-faced monkey clutching a piece of apple with his fingers. The couple explained to Mr. Andrews that they could no longer keep Ricky, that he was becoming a very mean little monkey, and they were too old to handle him. They practically begged him to take Ricky.

As they left, the man said, "Oh, and he can be a little nippy at times."

They quickly got into the car and sped down the driveway, gravel and dust flying behind them.

Ricky became part of the family. He lived in a large walk-in cage made comfortable for a little monkey. Often Mr. Andrews would let him out, and Ricky would follow him around the farm. He loved to play in the old ficus tree, and he would swing from the branches, entertaining the waiting families and their children. Mr. Andrews kept a watchful eye on him while he was out of the cage.

Everyone who kept their horses at the barn were kind, friendly folks. As the neighborhood around them grew, the farm stayed the same. The neighbors liked the farm and its animals, and they especially liked the Andrews family. It was a surprise when one day a man named Mr. Jensen drove up to the barn and confronted Mr. Andrews under the big tree.

"I live over on 112th Street in the Pine Grove area," he said.

Mr. Andrews shook his hand and said, "Nice to meet you, sir."

Mr. Jensen was a fierce-looking man, whose scowl and raised voice kept everyone else at a distance. He complained about the smell of the farm, the dogs that barked so loudly in the morning, kids yelling, and horses neighing. He had nothing nice to say, but Mr. Andrews just listened.

"Didn't you realize that Pine Grove was built right next to a farm when you bought your house?" Mr. Andrews asked kindly.

"Well, yes!" roared Mr. Jensen. "But I didn't expect this amount of noise and the smell is horrendous."

Since Mr. Andrews spoke so intently with this neighbor, he didn't realize that Ricky had moved from the tree to the ground and that the little monkey was looking quizzically at Mr. Jensen. Before he could be lifted away from the angry man, Ricky did an awful thing. He pulled up Mr. Jensen's pants leg and bit right into his hairy white calf, causing drops of blood to appear.

"Ow!" screamed Mr. Jensen. The louder the man screamed, the more tightly that monkey latched onto his leg, and he wouldn't let go—a bad situation that got worse by the minute. Finally, Ricky let go of the man's pants leg and scooted back up into the tree as fast as a little monkey could.

"What the heck was that?" screamed the angry man.

"Uh, our monkey, sir'" replied Mr. Andrews. "I'm so sorry. Let me help you with that."

"I hope that monkey had his shots!" bellowed Mr. Jensen.

"Yes, he did, but let's go to the house and see if we can clean it up," said Mr. Andrews.

"No, I'm going to my doctor," he replied as he was calming down. And before either could say another word, Mr. Jensen hopped in his car and left. Mr. Andrews never heard from him again.

Chapter 7

Halloween Parade

On the way home from school one pleasant October day, Hilary's sister Sara talked about the upcoming Halloween parade. This was a favorite among the riders at the Andrews farm. They would dress up their horses and themselves in the most imaginative costumes and parade around the farm. Those who chose to participate entered the big horse show as a team in the costume class.

Sara enjoyed helping the riders create the costumes. She didn't care for riding as much as drawing, painting, and creating. She chose ideas, patterns, and colors, and she was anxious for the planning to begin. Thankfully, it was weeks away, but a group of riders met together to discuss their plans for the parade. Sally wanted to be a witch, and with her big, ebony horse, that would be perfect.

"I already have a witch's hat and some old fake fingernails," she said.

Joey wanted to dress up like a scarecrow, and he showed them how he could dance like a limp, floppy mop around his pony. Hilary wanted to be a princess with a silver crown and a sparkly silver scepter.

"I could put sparkles and stars all over Holly," she thought.

"Wait!" cried Sara. "Does this sound like one of my favorite movies to you?" The others were puzzled but Sara continued, "Sally can be the Wicked Witch of the West; Hilary can be Glinda the good witch; Joey can be the scarecrow."

"I want to be Dorothy," replied Franny. They had a plan.

The day came when the practice parade was held on the farm. It was late October, and it was starting to feel a little cooler. The trees held onto their green leaves and not much had changed around them except for the excitement building up for the big South Miami horse show. Families spent hours creating costumes for their riders and ponies or horses. The Andrews family found time to devote to that too. Sara handled the costume details for her sisters. Then one Saturday afternoon, Mr. Andrews fixed up the picnic area with chairs for the parents, and the riders paraded past, fully dressed in costume.

"Presenting the winning team of the costume class, we hope!" yelled Sara.

First Franny rode by in a blue checkered dress, red shoes, and pigtails. She carried a basket with one of the Andrews terriers safely tucked inside of it. Cocoa was dressed up like a lion, her beautiful mane completely frizzed and her long tail tied together with a puff on the end. One friend dressed in a metal-looking tin woodsman costume, and her horse was covered with red poppies. Joey was dancing around his horse, jumping on and off as he walked. He wore a plaid shirt and old denim jeans stuffed with hay. Sally rode in as the wicked witch, with a dark pointy witch's hat and a long black cape. Her face and hands were painted green, warts and all. On her back rested Ricky, with little wings that bobbed up and down. He was clearly having the time of his life for a curious little monkey.

"I'll get you, my pretty!" cackled Sally, waving her cape across her horse's neck.

Then came Hilary on her pony, Holly. Wearing a white chiffon dress, long white gloves, and a silver crown, she looked just as a good witch should. Her hair was long and wavy with sparkly gems and little silver stars. What fun!

"The good witch should have a gray or white horse," said Joey.

"I was thinking the same thing," suggested Mr. Andrews.

"I have an idea," said Mrs. Andrews, and she hurried back into the barn.

"What's up?" said Hilary.

She stared in amazement as out of the barn stepped the most beautiful creature. He was decorated in silvery painted spots from head to hoof, and his mane was braided with cerulean blue ribbons woven in and around it. Small silver stars came out of the crown piece on his bridle. His tail was pure white, long and flowing, with matching blue sparkles. Everyone gasped at once.

"Chipper!" Hilary cried.

"We thought we'd surprise you," said her mom.

Sara said, "Doesn't he look like royalty?" Hilary had to agree that he did and that his gray dapples were perfect for the costume. Sara's face lit up with pride as they all admired her work.

But as Hilary climbed off Holly's back and onto Chipper, she felt some regret.

"Sorry, Holly" she said. "I still love you."

The suggestion was made to let one of the students ride Holly dressed as a munchkin.

Hilary's long dress fell over Chipper's back. She felt like a princess as she collected the reins, stroked his neck, and sat comfortably on his bare back. Chipper's neck was arched and his ears perked. He started to jig in place, ready to move.

"Calm down," whispered Hilary. "I'll let you know when I'm ready." At that moment she realized that she was in control of her fears and needed to instill in her horse that she was his partner and they were in this together.

The parents cheered as the riders paraded around the ring. After carefully putting their horses and costumes away, they joined everyone for homemade cookies, apples, and punch under the old tree. Even Ricky snatched an apple and climbed up to the highest branch. The parents commented on the elaborate costumes, and they agreed to take all the students to the show to compete in the costume class. Perhaps they would win a blue ribbon. But if not, it was still great fun and everyone would get to help.

Chapter 8

Goats

In the evenings, Mr. Andrews let Nanny and Billy out of the goat pasture so they could roam around the farm. Even though they usually just followed him around, they were much more mischievous than Ricky. Goats and monkey were not let loose at the same time.

Nothing can come between a goat and its stomach. Nanny and Billy nibbled on everything from fallen mulberries to leftover hay to children's clothing. Nibbling on clothing was more out of curiosity than to satisfy their hunger. They were very sociable and loved visiting the people on the farm. The goats liked to explore and tended to wander off on their own.

Between two of the paddocks on the farm was a concrete watering trough. Inside the trough were three plump goldfish that helped to keep it clean. Hilary was taking a riding lesson from Jenny in one of the paddocks, riding Chipper over two of the jumps, practicing without reins. The reins were knotted and rested on Chipper's neck. Hilary's outstretched arms guided him over the jumps with her leg signals. She trotted around the paddock and came back to jump again and again, each time doing something different. First she rode without reins, then without stirrups, then with eyes closed and hands on her head. These exercises helped instill confidence, poise, and strength.

Meanwhile, the two goats climbed up on the water trough and were chewing grass and eyeing the goldfish. Billy butted at Nanny to push her off, and she hopped right back up again and again. Mr. Andrews came over to shoo them away as he watched Hilary riding through the exercises.

"Great job!" he called.

Jenny smiled and said, "How about this pair? Aren't they doing excellent work?"

Hilary was feeling so much more sure of herself that she planned to enter Chipper into some of the equitation classes at the show. Mr. Andrews gave them a thumbs-up and walked away to finish his chores. At the end of the lesson, Hilary walked Chipper around until he cooled down.

"Just drop your reins and let him relax," said Jenny.

Hilary kicked off her stirrups and relaxed, too. She started over to the trough to give Chipper a drink of water when … *splash!* Nanny fell right into the water and was squealing like a pig. Billy jumped off and quickly backed up away from the scene. But Nanny was stuck. Her back leg was wedged between the fence and the trough, and half of her body was in the water. Her head was thrashing back and forth, and her squeals were ear-piercing.

Jenny and Mr. Andrews ran to help her. Suddenly, Chipper regained his energy and scooted away from the commotion as quickly as possible, breaking into a canter. Hilary wasn't prepared for that. She stayed on his back, grabbed up her reins, pulled back, and brought him to a halt. She turned him to face the goat calamity then patted his neck. His ears were perked and his tail was up in the air as he tossed his head.

"For Pete's sake, Chipper, it's just a goat!" Hilary said as she felt her heart beating wildly.

"You silly goat," said Mr. Andrews as he dragged Nanny out of the water.

"That's not something I was expecting," Hilary said, breathing hard.

"Horses are full of surprises," said Mr. Andrews.

Nanny bleated: "Baa-baa!"

"And so are goats!" Mr. Andrews added with a laugh.

"You really handled that well," replied Jenny. "Now hop off and cool him down, then we'll look at the classes for the show."

They met at the picnic table on the gravel beneath the ficus tree. Jenny pulled the crumpled list out of her back pocket.

"Let's check out the young riders' section," said Jenny.

"I'm riding only in equitation classes, right?" replied Hilary.

"Yes, I think it's best to focus on that for now," Jenny added. She explained to Hilary what the word equitation means in addition to just riding on horseback.

"In a horse show, the rider is judged on the use of riding aids like your hands and legs, also on form, and even the correct attire or clothing. The rider, horse, bridle, and saddle should be clean and present a polished look," Jenny explained.

"Can you help me braid Chipper's mane?" asked Hilary.

"Sure," said Jenny. "I'll teach you how to use thread to hold the braids."

Hilary couldn't stop smiling as she hopped on the table and put her feet on the bench. Jenny took her big straw hat off and fanned herself with it as they read.

South Miami Horse Show
Hunter Seat Equitation Classes
Sunday, 9:00 a.m.
Equitation 11 and under, flat
Equitation 11 and under, fences 2'3"
Equitation 12–14, flat
Equitation 12–14, fences 3'
Equitation 15–17, flat
Equitation 15–17, fences 3'6"

Short stirrup equitation w/t
Short stirrup equitation w/t/c
Short stirrup equitation, fences 18"
Special Costume class

"Can I ride in the short stirrup classes?" asked Hilary.

Jenny replied: "I think you've outgrown those, Hil. You are better qualified for the eleven and under division, and you can certainly jump the fences at two feet three inches."

Although Hilary felt a little anxious, she said, "Let's do it!"

Franny came to sit next to Jenny. She leaned into her lap and asked, "What's flat mean?"

"Riding on the flat means there are no jumps involved," answered Jenny.

"And how about w/t/c?" Franny asked.

"Walk, trot, and canter," Hilary said.

"When can I show Cocoa?" Franny begged, batting her eyelashes at Jenny.

"Soon, Franny," Jenny replied, smiling.

It had been a long day, and the girls were ready for dinner.

"Race you to the house!" yelled Franny as she took off down the path.

"That girl has way too much energy," Hilary said to herself.

Chapter 9

The Big Day

The night before the show, the Andrews family polished off a delicious dinner of chicken, rice, and salad,
with brownies for dessert. The girls helped clean up
the kitchen, and Mr. Andrews checked on the barn.
Sara and Franny were in bed by eight o'clock. Hilary
was in bed by nine. Wearing her cozy nightgown, she
pulled the blanket up to her chin. As she dozed off, she
dreamed about the day ahead.

The barn was pleasantly silent except for the rus-
tling of hay or clinking of a halter on a water bucket.
Some stray hens were pecking at grain on the floor,
and one was nestled in the corner of a stall, ruffling her
feathers into the hay. The barn cats were nibbling at
dry food that Franny left out for them. The riders spent
the day riding, washing, grooming, and clipping their
horses. Their fetlocks and bridle paths were trimmed.

Tack was cleaned; bits were polished. Now the horses stood quietly in the stalls, enjoying the peace.

"Every single creature on the farm is quiet," said Mr. Andrews to his wife as they sat and drank sweet tea on the porch that evening.

"I think they're all worn out," she replied. "I know I am."

"We'd better call it a night too," said Mr. Andrews as he hugged Mrs. Andrews. "It will be quite a day tomorrow."

When morning came, they got up at daylight, had cereal for breakfast, and put on old clothes to finish their work. The horses were fed, watered, and groomed once again. Hilary and some of the other riders braided their horses' manes and polished their own boots. Chickens fluttered around spilled oats, and parents helped their children to prepare. It was a busy time. Fitz chased a barn cat right up into the hayloft. Mr. Andrews prepared the horse trailer with fresh hay in nets and water buckets for the horses. Saddles and bridles were loaded into the old station wagon. Mr. Andrews made a few trips delivering horses and riders to the show grounds, which was just four miles away. Hilary watched as a young girl dressed in jodhpurs, a T-shirt, and boots walked Holly onto the trailer ramp. She was happy for the girl, and she knew that Holly would take good care of her at the show.

Chipper needed an extra scrubbing on his gray belly before Hilary loaded him onto the ramp. She felt butterflies in her own belly as they approached the fairgrounds. As they pulled into the fairgrounds, they heard music and smelled the dust and straw of the stables. There were two rings—one was filled with a course of jumps and the other was empty. While Chipper was being unloaded, he perked up his ears and looked around, holding his head high.

"Time to practice in the warm-up ring," said Jenny. When you're ready, meet me in the big ring.

Hilary saddled and bridled Chipper and gave him one last brushing. In the back of the trailer, she finished putting on her riding clothes and helmet while her dad held Chipper. Then she made her way over to the ring. Another horse trailer rattled down the path, and music blared from the stand between announcements. The aroma of coffee and fresh doughnuts drifted by as they passed the food truck. In the ring, around and around they went, first at a trot and then at a canter, in both directions. Hilary was feeling a little less nervous but anxious for her class to begin. Jenny walked alongside Hilary in the ring.

Jenny said, "Remember: heels down, eyes up, and quiet hands. If he speeds up, just make a circle and try to stay away from other riders."

"Schooling time is over. Please leave the ring," called the voice over the public address system.

They left as the big watering truck pulled into the ring to dampen the dirt and dust. Mrs. Andrews gave Hilary's boots one last polish with a rag and hugged her daughter's waist.

"Good luck! This will be fun!" she said cheerfully. Hilary hoped she was right. Her mom was always so positive. They stood and chatted for a few more minutes until the class was about to begin. Her class was the first of the day: equitation for riders eleven and under, on the flat.

The judge took her place with a clipboard in the center of the ring, and the announcer began calling riders to start the first class. So much was going through her mind, but Hilary felt strong and trusted Chipper to do his best. *Heels down, hands quiet, eyes up, check your diagonal.* Her heart was pounding as she walked into the ring. Riders jogged around the ring, instructors gave last minute advice from the sidelines, and the gate was closed.

Showtime! Would Chipper shy at that big awning flapping in the wind over the hamburger stand or at the prize ribbons fluttering on the judge's stand? Hilary reminded herself to relax. After all, Chipper was very experienced in showing, even though this was only Hilary's fifth show in her life. After a few times around the ring of trotting and walking, they changed directions at a walk.

Then the announcer called: "All right, riders, canter!"

Hilary gently turned her horse's head to the inside of the ring and squeezed with her outside leg. Chipper gracefully leaned into a canter on the correct lead. Whew! Just like a rocking horse, they cantered around the ring twice until the announcer called for them to walk. The next request was that the riders drop their stirrups while posting to a trot. One rider immediately lost her grip and slipped off onto the grassy area of the ring. Her pony stood and watched her as she led him back to the center. Hilary was glad she had practiced this a lot while on the farm. Just then, coming around the corner outside the far end of the ring, came a huge yellow watering truck with its fenders clanking and engine sputtering. While rounding the corner, it back-fired twice. Two of the ponies scooted away from the rail, upsetting their riders' balance. Chipper perked up his ears. He snorted and sped up just a little.

"It's okay, boy. Stay calm," Hilary whispered. She reached down and stroked his neck, and by the time they were at the opposite end of the ring, he was focused and steady. Hilary breathed a sigh of relief. Then the class was asked to line up so the judge could see them one last time. The judge walked in and out of the line between the riders, using her clipboard to record last-minute observations. As she approached Chipper,

Hilary thought that she was going to tell her something went wrong.

But the judge walked up and patted Chipper's neck and said, "You did a great job, and what a lovely horse."

Hilary's heart just swelled with pride. No matter what the results, she knew she had tried her best. The crackling of the speakers brought Hilary back to the present. Then she was amazed!

"And first place in the equitation class is Miss Hilary Andrews on Blue Chip!" called the announcer. Blue Chip was Chipper's show name. Mrs. Andrews chose his name because it was a sign of good luck. Everyone called him Chipper. The stunning silver trophy was handed to Hilary, and the blue ribbon was clipped to his bridle. She sat tall in the saddle as she accepted with a big thank you. Her goal was to do her best, remain calm, and stay on Chipper's back! She never even thought of winning first prize. Second, third, fourth, and fifth places were announced, but Hilary barely heard the results. She was on cloud nine!

"I knew you could do it!" cried Sally.

"Terrific job!" called Mr. and Mrs. Andrews, who hugged Hilary as she dismounted.

Jenny held the horse's reins, gave Hilary a hug too, and told her how proud she was of her accomplishment. "I thought when Chipper heard and saw that water truck that he would try something sneaky," laughed Jenny.

"Me too!" cried Hilary.

Happy as ever, this was her first ribbon with Chipper, and it was a blue.

Later, back at the trailer, horses crunched carrots, nibbled on hay, and pulled at their leads to get to grass. Riders were grooming, braiding, or otherwise preparing for their classes. Hilary was busy getting ready for her next class, equitation over fences.

"Let's go!" said Mr. Andrews. "You're the fifth rider on the course."

She hopped on Chipper again, adjusted his girth, and checked to see that everything was in place. Mrs. Andrews fixed Hilary's hair, which was pulled to the back of her helmet with a long braid and a small shamrock green bow at the end of it that matched her coat. She wore tan jodhpurs with laced brown paddock boots. She felt very polished indeed.

Jenny met them at the warm-up ring, where riders were trotting over a post and rail jump one at a time. Instructors mingled in the middle, guiding their riders with last-minute instructions. Hilary looked over the course of jumps, which was posted near the in-gate. The course looked easy. It was twice around the outside and down the middle. They watched as two riders rode the course very smoothly. Hilary took one last jump in the warm-up ring before her number was called.

"Number twenty-three, Hilary Andrews riding Blue Chip!" called the announcer.

Hilary trotted Chipper into the ring, his head raised and alert as she trotted a wide circle in front of the first fence, a striped post and rail jump. As Hilary sat deep in her saddle, Chipper picked up his canter, and she leaned forward as they headed toward the rails. She gave him a light squeeze with her legs, and he knew enough to do the rest, finding the exact spot to take off and land on the other side. Straight ahead came the bushy green brush jump, then down the other side over the small coop and another rail fence. Hilary looked ahead to her next fence, passed Jenny along the sidelines, and rode into the blue striped rails once again, then up and over. Counting the strides between the jumps, Hilary expected Chipper to approach the brush jump again just as before. Just then—a big surprise! A child on the sidelines decided to throw a large paper wrapper out into the ring, and it landed right in front of the brush jump. That spooked Chipper, and he stopped abruptly with his feet planted firmly in the ground right in front of the fence.

"Okay, buddy let's try it again," said Hilary. She made a tight circle to the left, picked up a canter again, and he sailed high over the brush, as if the paper wrapper was going to eat him alive. Then, looking to the left, Hilary finished with the big cross rail and barrel jump down the middle of the ring. Applause spread throughout the crowd as Hilary slowed to a trot, then to a walk.

"You did just as you should," Jenny said, patting Hilary's knee.

"What a surprise," sighed Hilary. "I didn't expect that."

"None of us did," replied Mrs. Andrews. "I'm impressed that you stayed on his back."

The other riders completed the course while Hilary watched. Jenny encouraged her to learn from watching others ride. Hilary didn't expect to be in the ribbons this time, but maybe next time. She leaned over Chipper's neck and hugged him as she swung down to the ground. He turned his head to her and she could feel his warm, soft breath on her hand.

"You tricked me, buddy, but next time I'll be ready for anything to happen," she whispered.

He rubbed his dusty head on her riding jacket and searched her pocket for treats.

"I have some apples for you back at the trailer," she said.

She led Chipper back through the crowd, past hurried riders, parents carrying armfuls of their riders' belongings, and past the hot dog stand. Hilary's stomach started to growl from the smell of hot dogs and popcorn. Back at the trailer, she unsaddled Chipper and used a bucket of water and a sponge to wipe away the saddle marks. Then she put on his halter and found a big, juicy golden delicious, took a bite, and gave the rest to Chipper.

"Dad, may I get a hot dog, and will you watch Chipper for me?" asked Hilary.

"Sure," said Mr. Andrews. "How about getting me a couple dogs too, with mustard? But make sure you come back within the hour. It will be time to bring out the costumes before you know it," he reminded her with a smile.

In the flat ring, it was time for the annual costume class, a tradition at the South Miami show. Teams of riders had such clever, colorful costumes. There were pumpkins, ghosts, and goblins. People laughed, whistled, and applauded. When the Andrews team rode into the ring, the crowd went wild. They placed first in the costume class, each rider receiving a blue ribbon. The scarecrow danced, the cowardly lion shook her head, Toto barked, and the wicked witch cackled. Franny sat straight and tall on Cocoa the lion, her pigtails sticking out with big blue bows. Sara walked with Franny and Cocoa because Franny could not be trusted to stay in line. She giggled and swung her pigtails around and clicked her ruby slippers up over Cocoa's head. It's a good thing Cocoa was a sweet, gentle horse. Someone decided it might be better if Sara carried the basket with Toto because he was barking at everything. The good witch and her sparkly gray steed brought up the end of the line, and Hilary waved her silver wand to the crowd. Sally's mom came into the ring and took a picture of the Andrews farm crew.

"Now you're off to see the wizard!" she sang. Sally's mom was great fun.

They all left the ring smiling and cheering.

Hilary rode Chipper back to the trailer. Sara helped Franny with her costume, and then they both helped Hilary. Parents joined their riders and chatted about how great the costumes looked.

"Toto even barked!" laughed Sara.

"And you make a great wicked witch," said Sally's mom to her daughter. Sally just winked at Hilary.

"Maybe that's because I know what a wicked witch looks like," she chuckled.

"Shh!" admonished Hilary.

Near day's end, the fair grounds were soon deserted, and riders were packing up their belongings. Trailers slowly ambled down the road. The stable area was still littered with bits of hay and a few horse show flyers while people cleaned the area. They loaded Chipper and Holly into the trailer, and Mrs. Andrews offered Hilary a bottle of water.

"I'm so proud of you," she said. "You had faith in your horse and in all of the hard work you've done together."

"I couldn't have done it without everyone's help and support," said Hilary as she hugged Chipper and Holly. She gave them extra carrots and bran mash that night for dinner. It was a long, rewarding day.

Chapter 10

The Day After

Hilary spent the entire day in school daydreaming about the horse show and her blue ribbon win on Chipper. She pictured the shiny trophy and the silky blue ribbon hanging in her room. She pictured her "lovely" horse (as the judge described him) trotting gracefully around the ring, his mane and tail perfectly braided, his dappled gray coat, and ears so alert. She thought of the way her dad shined her boots right before she went in the ring and the way her mom fixed her hair and her helmet. She remembered last-minute instructions from Jenny and friends cheering for her. It had taken time to get used to riding Chipper, but now each time she rode him, she felt more relaxed.

The day after a horse show was always a day of rest for the horses. Hilary watched as a new friend offered Holly a special treat of sugar cubes. The family decided that they would keep Holly as a lesson pony for young riders and that she would grow old on the farm. Hilary was looking forward to future competitions with Chipper. She hopped up on him and rode bareback out to the mulberry trees, with just a halter and lead rope to guide him. As she settled down under the trees, she heard Sally's voice.

"Wait up!" Sally called. She came trotting up on her horse to join Hilary.

"Now we can both reach the mulberries more easily," said Hilary.

"Unless … you want to go next door and buy a basket of raspberries," Sally said with a laugh. "I could really go for some of your mom's raspberry cobbler."